JIP and JAM and the MISSING STICK

By Elizabeth Scully

CHAPTER 1

Jam has a stick.

It is a big stick.

Jam can lift it up.

Jam can run with it.

Jip did not get a stick.

Can Jip get a big stick?

Can Jip get the stick from Jam?

Jam bit the stick.

Jip can not get it from Jam.

Jam lifts the stick up and runs.

CHAPTER 2

Jam hid the big stick.

Can Jip get the big stick?

Is it up on the bed?

Is it at the sink?

Is it in the grass?

Where is the big stick?

Jip wants to get it!

Jip will look in the tub.
Is the big stick in the tub?

Yes! It is in the tub!

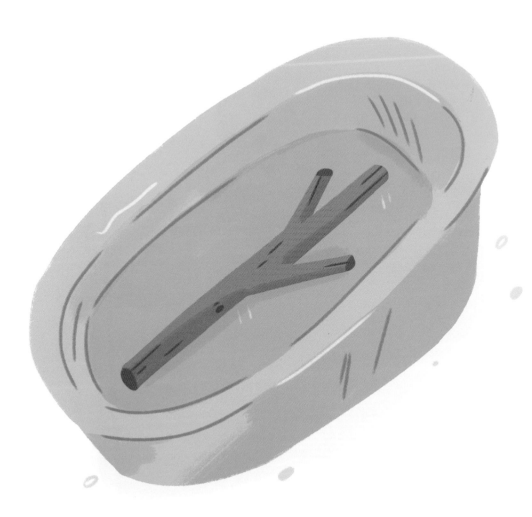

Jip got it! Jip got the big stick.

WORD LIST

sight words

a	the
at	to
from	wants
look	Where

consonant digraphs

/k/ck	**/s/ss**
stick	grass
/l/ll	**/th/th**
will	with

120 WORDS

Jam has a stick.
It is a big stick.
Jam can lift it up. Jam can run with it.
Jip did not get a stick.
Can Jip get a big stick?
Can Jip get the stick from Jam?
Jam bit the stick.
Jip can not get it from Jam.
Jam lifts the stick up and runs.

Jam hid the big stick.
Can Jip get the big stick?
Is it up on the bed?
Is it at the sink?
Is it in the grass?
Where is the big stick?
Jip wants to get it!
Jip will look in the tub. Is the big stick
in the tub?
Yes! It is in the tub!
Jip got it! Jip got the big stick.

Published in the United States of America by Cherry Lake Publishing Group
Ann Arbor, Michigan
www.cherrylakepublishing.com

Illustrator: Laura Gomez
Book Designer: Melinda Millward

Graphic Element Credits: Cover, multiple interior pages: © memej/Shutterstock, © Eka
Panova/Shutterstock, © Pand P Studio/Shutterstock, © PRebellion Works/Shutterstock

Cherry Blossom Press is an imprint of Cherry Lake Publishing Group.

Library of Congress Cataloging-in-Publication Data has been filed
and is available at catalog.loc.gov

Cherry Lake Publishing Group would like to acknowledge the work of the
Partnership for 21st Century Learning, a Network of Battelle for Kids.
Please visit http://www.battelleforkids.org/networks/p21 for more information.

Printed in the United States of America
Corporate Graphics

Note from publisher: Websites change regularly, and their future contents are
outside of our control. Supervise children when conducting any recommended
online searches for extended learning opportunities.